W9-CQH-451

Monster
of the
Year

YOUNG YEARLING BOOKS YOU WILL ENJOY:

The Pee Wee Scout books by Judy Delton

Cookies and Crutches
Camp Ghost-Away
Lucky Dog Days
Blue Skies, French Fries
Grumpy Pumpkins
Peanut-Butter Pilgrims

A Pee Wee Christmas
That Mushy Stuff
Spring Sprouts
The Pooped Troop
The Pee Wee Jubilee

The Polka Dot Private Eye books by Patricia Reilly Giff

The Mystery of the Blue Ring
The Riddle of the Red Purse
The Secret at the Polk Street School
The Powder Puff Puzzle

The Case of the Cool-Itch Kid
Garbage Juice for Breakfast
The Trail of the Screaming Teenager
The Clue at the Zoo

Yearling Books/Young Yearlings/Yearling Classics are designed especially to entertain and enlighten young people. Patricia Reilly Giff, consultant to this series, received the bachelor's degree from Marymount College. She holds the master's degree in history from St. John's University, and a Professional Diploma in Reading from Hofstra University. She was a teacher and reading consultant for many years, and is the author of numerous books for young readers.

For a complete listing of all Yearling titles, write to
Dell Readers Service, P.O. Box 1045,
South Holland, IL 60473.

Monster of the Year

◆

Stephen Mooser

Illustrated by George Ulrich

A YOUNG YEARLING BOOK

Published by
Dell Publishing
a division of
Bantam Doubleday Dell Publishing Group, Inc.
666 Fifth Avenue
New York, New York 10103

Text copyright © 1990 by Stephen Mooser
Illustrations copyright © 1990 by George Ulrich

All rights reserved. No part of this book may be reproduced or transmitted in any form or by any means, electronic or mechanical, including photocopying, recording, or by any information storage and retrieval system, without the written permission of the Publisher, except where permitted by law.

The trademark Yearling® is registered in the U.S. Patent and Trademark Office.

The trademark Dell® is registered in the U.S. Patent and Trademark Office.

ISBN: 0-440-40363-4

Printed in the United States of America

September 1990

10 9 8 7 6 5 4 3 2 1

CWO

*For
Violet Ginsburg*

Contents

◆

Chapter 1

♦

Monster of the Year

"**I** hope you've enjoyed my vampire speech," said the monster to Ms. Hatfield's class. "Maybe you've even learned something."

He was the ugliest monster most of the students had ever seen. So ugly that some of them could barely look at his bulging yellow eyes. Or his face full of leaky green warts. "And now, my friends," continued the monster, "I'd like to close with a joke. My sister said that for her birthday she'd like a surprise. I said okay. Here it is.... BOO!"

Ms. Hatfield's class laughed and clapped their hands. The monster bowed. Then he took off his mask. It was Melvin Purdy. With his big ears and his checkered pants he didn't look very scary. In fact, he looked a little scared himself. Quickly, he hurried back to his desk and sat down.

"That was a nice speech," said Ms. Hatfield. It was a Monday. Everyone knew that by looking at their teacher's tennis shoes, black-and-white ones. Low tops. She wore different sneakers on each day. "And I thought it was nice that you wore that mask. It fit right in with your monster theme."

"Melvin was elected Monster of the Year by the Creepy Creature Club," said Henry Potter. He puffed out his skinny chest. "Last year I was the one that got elected."

"The Monster of the Year gets to wear the special creepy creature mask," said Melvin. "We like scary things." He looked down at the mask and gulped. "As long as they're not too scary."

Ms. Hatfield knew all about the Creepy Creature Club. Many of its members were in her class. The Creepy Creatures was a club for people who read ghost stories, went to scary movies, and collected monster cards. They met in a garage decorated like a haunted house.

Ms. Hatfield rubbed her hands together. "You know the school is having an election this week too," she said. "Someone is going to be the new school president. Every class gets to nominate someone. During the week the candidates will speak to some of the classes. Then, on Friday, everyone who is running will speak to a school assembly. Afterward everyone votes." Ms. Hatfield smiled. "The best speaker usually wins."

"Nominate me," said Henry. He patted down a feather of hair that was sticking up in back. "I'm the most popular kid in school. I'll get all the votes."

Everyone laughed. Henry was always bragging.

"I'm sorry, Henry. You can't run," said Ms. Hatfield. "Remember. You ran last year."

"And you only got ten votes," said Melvin. "Remember?"

Henry turned and glared at Melvin. "Do you think you could do better?"

"Well ... I—I ..." said Melvin, stuttering.

"Well," said Henry, "go on. Could you?"

"Of course he could," said Rosa Dorado. She was seated behind Henry too. She had long black hair and big brown eyes. "Lots of people would vote for Melvin. And he's a good speaker too."

"But I don't—" began Melvin.

"I can't believe it," said Henry, cutting

3

him off. He turned and faced the class. "You really think Melvin would get more votes than me?"

"Easy," said Rosa.

"But," said Melvin, "I'm not a very good—"

"Melvin," said Rosa, interrupting, "believe in yourself. If you want to be president, nothing can stop you."

He looked desperately around the room. "But don't you see I . . ."

Henry snorted with disgust. "I won't try to stop you, Melvin. If you want to be a big shot, go ahead. Run."

"Let's vote," said Rosa. She turned to the class. "Everybody who wants Melvin to run, raise their hand."

Everybody raised a hand. Everybody but Melvin.

"You're on your way," said Rosa. She gave Melvin a little salute. "You're a great Monster of the Year. But you're going to be an even better school president. I'm glad you decided to run."

"But—" whined Melvin.

"You're going to learn a lot," said Ms. Hatfield. "Speaking in public is a good skill to have. Tomorrow morning you'll give your first speech."

Melvin felt a shiver. Speeches scared him silly. Nervously he chewed on his thumb.

"It won't be hard," said Ms. Hatfield. "Tomorrow you only have to talk to the kindergarten. It will be good practice for Friday's assembly."

"But what if the kindergartners laugh. Or call me names," said Melvin. "Talking in front of people scares me."

"Talking scares you?" said Ms. Hatfield. She peered over her glasses. "I don't understand. You just gave a wonderful speech. And you weren't nervous at all."

"That's because it was the monster talking, not me," said Melvin. He stared down at his desk. "Can I wear the mask tomorrow?"

"That mask might scare the little kids," said Ms. Hatfield. "You'll have to ask their teacher, Mr. Libby."

"Don't worry. Mr. Libby will let you wear it," said Henry. He crossed his fingers and held them up. "Libby and I are that close. I'll talk to him for you. No sweat."

"Henry, you just have to," said Melvin. "If I can't wear that mask, I'll freeze up for sure."

Henry reached over and poked Melvin in the nose.

"Just let me take it from here," he said. "I'm going to teach you how to be a great speaker." He patted down his feather of hair and grinned. "Someday maybe you'll even be as good as me."

"But, Henry . . ." whined Melvin.

"No buts," said Henry. "If I can't be president, then I want to make sure that my Creepy Creature friend gets it. By the time I'm done, you'll be a star."

Melvin gulped. "Me?"

Henry made a fist. He punched Melvin in the shoulder. "And after you become school president, we'll run for mayor."

"Mayor?" said Melvin.

"After that it will be governor, then senator." Henry sighed. He put his hands behind his head and leaned back. "Before long you'll be president of the whole country."

Melvin rubbed his fist against his cheek. "But I'm no good at giving speeches."

"Nonsense," said Henry. "You just gave a great speech. Remember what Rosa said, believe in yourself. That's your first lesson."

Melvin looked around the room. Everyone was staring. He didn't know how it happened. But it had. He was running for president. For better or for worse.

He looked over at Henry. Henry smiled and rubbed his hands together. "I got big plans for you," he said.

Melvin groaned. No doubt about it now. It was going to be for the worse.

Chapter 2

◆

I Scream Surprise

Lunch that day was hot dogs, french fries, and ice cream. Melvin took his food and sat down by himself. He wanted to be alone. He needed time to think. Besides, he loved hot dogs, french fries, and ice cream. And he wanted to enjoy lunch in peace.

"Ah! There you are," said Henry Potter. He slapped Melvin on the back and sat down. "How's the new president?"

"President?" said Melvin.

"It's just a matter of time," said Henry. He winked and pinned a blue paper star on Melvin's shirt. "What do you think of this? I made it just for you."

Melvin looked down at the star. It said: VOTE FOR MELVIN. HE'LL MAKE A PURDY GOOD PRESIDENT.

"Purdy good slogan, huh?" said Henry.

Purdy dumb, thought Melvin. He sighed. It didn't look as if lunch was going to be very peaceful.

"We have lots of work to do," said Henry. He took a big bite of his hot dog. "We have to get ready for tomorrow's speech."

Melvin shivered. He'd been trying to forget about the speech.

Henry's mouth was filled with hot dog. But that didn't stop him from talking. "You'll begin with a joke. That's a good way to start a speech."

"It is?" said Melvin.

"Sure," mumbled Henry. "It relaxes your audience. And it will relax you too."

Melvin rubbed his fist against his cheek. "But what if no one laughs?"

Henry drowned his french fries in catsup. "Why did the monster cross the road?" he asked.

Melvin shook his head. "I don't know."

"So that he could eat the chicken on the other side!" Henry laughed. A bit of hot dog squirted out of his mouth.

Melvin turned away.

"Pretty funny, huh?" said Henry. He slapped Melvin on the back. "The kindergartners will love it. You'll get their votes for sure."

Melvin didn't think the joke was very funny. But maybe little kids would.

"And another thing," said Henry. He grabbed a handful of messy french fries and shoved them into his mouth. "You've got to look cool. Tomorrow morning I'll bring you some new pants."

Melvin looked down at his pants. They were covered with red and black squares. They barely reached to his ankles. "What's wrong with these pants?" he asked.

Henry shoved another handful of fries into his mouth. "They look stupid," he said. "Do you want people to laugh at you?"

Melvin shook his head.

"To give a good speech you have to look good," said Henry. "That's another rule."

Melvin felt dizzy. There were so many rules. How could he remember them all? He picked up the bottle of catsup. He was starving. Henry was almost done eating. But he hadn't even started.

Before Melvin could shake the catsup onto his fries, someone came walking up.

"Purdy for president!" He heard someone laugh. "You know what that is? A purdy good joke!"

Melvin looked up. It was Zack Morton. He had a scrunched-up nose and a flattop.

He was the school bully. He was always fighting with the Creepy Creatures.

He was wearing an old leather jacket. Right on the front was written: ZACK FOR PRESIDENT. VOTE FOR ME. OR ELSE! It was written in ink.

"Drop out," snarled Zack. "You don't stand a chance. Everybody is going to vote for me. Or else."

"Or else what?" said Henry. His chin was covered with catsup.

Zack made a fist. "Or else they'll be sorry."

"You don't scare the Creepy Creatures," said Henry. "You can't hurt us."

"When I get elected, I'm going to make a rule that the Creepy Creatures can't have meetings at school. And they can't wear their costumes on special days either," said Zack. "That's my number-one promise."

Melvin's mouth fell open. "You couldn't do that. You wouldn't."

"The president can do anything he wants," said Zack. "Just watch me."

Melvin still had the catsup bottle in his hand, upside down. "I hope you don't win," he said in his squeaky voice.

"He won't win," said Henry. "He'll chicken out before he gives his speech. He talks big, but I bet he doesn't show up at the assembly."

"Don't make me laugh," said Zack. "Talk about chickens. Purdy is the biggest cluck-cluck in the school."

"I am not a cluck-cluck," mumbled Melvin.

Suddenly Zack poked Melvin in the forehead. "Drop out, Purdy. If you know what's good for you."

Henry pushed Zack's hand away. "Bug off," he said. "Melvin isn't afraid of you."

"Tha-that's right," said Melvin in a shaky voice. "You don't sc-sc-scare me."

"Oh, yeah?" said Zack. He laughed. "Then why did you just do that?"

"Do what?" said Melvin.

"That," said Zack. He pointed at Melvin's plate.

Melvin looked down. His stomach nearly turned a flip. He had just covered his ice cream with catsup.

Chapter 3

◆

All the Wrong Laughs

The next morning Melvin got to class early. He was standing by the fishbowl chewing on his thumb when Henry walked in wearing a tall black magician's top hat. Across the front, written in white ink, were the words: ABRACADABRA! WE'RE GOING TO TURN A PURDY INTO A PRESIDENT!

Melvin winced. Then winced again when he saw a pair of gray pants in Henry's hand.

"I hope those aren't for me," said Melvin, when Henry came over.

Henry tapped Melvin on the nose. "They're my best pair," he said, handing them to Melvin. "Here. Take them to the bathroom and put them on before class starts. I want you looking super sharp for the speech."

Melvin unrolled the pants and shook his head.

"What's wrong?" said Henry.

"Just look. They're way too long," said Melvin.

"We'll roll up the cuffs," said Henry. "No problem. Now, hurry. Go try them on."

Melvin sighed. He knew it was no use to argue with Henry. He took the pants to the bathroom and put them on. When he came back, he was holding up the pants with his hand. And the bottoms were dragging on the floor.

"You see," said Melvin. "They're too big."

"Nonsense. They just need some fixing," said Henry. He bent down and rolled up the cuffs. "You see? No problem."

The bell was about to ring. Students were hurrying into class.

Melvin stood near his desk, holding up his pants.

"They're too loose," he whined. "They're going to fall off."

"Don't be a worrywart," said Henry. "They look perfect. Trust me."

Melvin picked up the mask on his desk.

"Henry, I hope you talked to Mr. Libby," he said. "I hope he said I could wear my mask."

"Don't worry about old Libby," said Henry. He tipped his top hat. "I'll handle him."

16

"You'd better," said Melvin. "I'm real nervous."

Henry poked the blue star on Melvin's shirt. "A president can't afford to be nervous," he said. "Is your speech ready?"

Melvin rubbed his fist against his cheek. "Sort of," he said. "I was just going to say, 'Vote for me. I'm Melvin Purdy, a purdy good guy.'"

"That's great!" said Henry. He slapped Melvin on the back. "Did you practice your joke?"

Melvin drew in a deep breath. "Why did the monster cross the road?"

Henry winked. "I don't know. Why did the monster cross the road?"

"So that he could eat the chicken on the other side," said Melvin softly.

"That's funny!" said Rosa Dorado. She had stopped to listen to Melvin's joke. "I like that."

Melvin brightened. "You do?"

Rosa nodded.

"Gee," said Melvin. "Maybe talking to those kindergartners won't be so bad after all."

Suddenly Melvin felt a hand on his shoulder. He looked down and saw a pair of purple tennis shoes. High tops. He didn't have to look up. It was a Tuesday. And the hand on his shoulder belonged to his teacher, Ms. Hatfield.

"The kindergarten class is waiting," said Ms. Hatfield. "Is Henry going with you?"

"Of course," said Henry. He pointed to his hat. "I'm his manager."

Ms. Hatfield smiled. "You'd better hurry. They're expecting you."

"We'll be back in a second with all the kindergarten votes," said Henry. He took off his hat and waved it. "Wish us luck!"

The class clapped. Then out the door they went. Henry's arm was around Melvin's shoulder. And Melvin's hand was on his pants, making sure they didn't fall down.

Mr. Libby's kindergarten class was at the end of the hall. Melvin put on the mask. Then he and Henry poked their heads in the door. The little kids were all sitting on a rug. Mr. Libby was holding up a book and reading them a story.

Henry knocked. Mr. Libby looked over. So did the kids.

"Eeeee-yikes!" screamed a boy in the front.

"A monster!" screeched a little girl. She jumped to her feet and started running in circles. "Help! Help!"

18

Some others put their hands over their eyes and started crying.

Mr. Libby dashed to the door. In a moment he had Henry and Melvin back in the hallway.

"Melvin! What are you doing in that mask? You've scared all my students," he said.

Mr. Libby had a bushy mustache. It was so bushy that you couldn't see his mouth. Sometimes it was hard to tell if he was happy or mad. But not this time. He was definitely not happy.

Melvin took off the mask. "I'd like to wear it during the speech. Can I?"

"Certainly not," said Mr. Libby. "The kids would have nightmares for a month."

Melvin gulped. His knees felt wobbly.

"Henry!" he hissed.

"Huh?" said Henry.

Melvin held up two crossed fingers. "Go on. I thought you said ..."

"Said what?" said Mr. Libby.

"Nothing," said Henry. He put his hand on Melvin's shoulder. "Come on. You can give the speech without the mask." He took it from Melvin and set it on the floor. "You can do it. Believe in yourself."

Before Melvin could run, Henry had led him into the kindergarten room.

All the little kids were standing. They stared at Melvin but didn't say anything. Melvin stared back and nervously chewed on his thumb. He kept his other hand on his pants, making sure they didn't fall down.

Mr. Libby told the kids to sit down. Then he brought Melvin over to the rug.

"Boys and girls, this is Melvin Purdy. He's running for school president. He's going to tell you why you should vote for him."

Mr. Libby stepped aside. Melvin gulped and looked over at the door.

The kindergartners stared at Melvin. Some of them began to fidget.

"Melvin!" whispered Henry. "Go on. Tell your joke. Remember. It will relax you and your audience."

Melvin drew in a deep breath. He tried to relax. But he couldn't. His heart was pounding like a parade drum. And his legs were shaking like guitar strings. Plucked ones.

"Melvin! The joke!" whispered Henry.

Melvin took a deep breath. He forced a smile.

"Why did the chicken cross the road?" he asked.

"So that he could get to the other side!" the kindergartners shouted back.

Melvin gulped. His knees nearly buckled. He'd messed up the joke. He'd told it backwards!

"So that he could get to the other side!" the boys and girls kept shouting. "So that he could get to the other side!"

"No, no," said Melvin, shaking his head. "You're wrong. He crossed the road so that he could eat the monster."

Suddenly everyone was quiet. The kids scratched their heads.

"Huh?" said Mr. Libby. He tugged on his mustache. "I don't get it."

Melvin felt dizzy. The audience wasn't laughing. They weren't relaxed. And neither was he. Rats! Why didn't Mr. Libby let him wear the mask? The Monster of the Year could have told the joke right. Easy.

"Just go on," whispered Henry. "Go."

All Melvin heard was the word *go*. He looked again at the door. This time he let his feet make the decision.

"Vote for me!" he yelled. And with those words he headed for the hall.

He was in such a hurry that he forgot to hold on to his pants. Down they came like a curtain. Before he knew what had happened, they were around his ankles. And his underpants were showing.

"Whooo-eeee!" yelled all the little kids. Everyone pointed and laughed.

Melvin turned around at the door. His face was red as a stoplight. Without saying a word he hitched up his pants and hopped out into the hall. He had never been so embarrassed. Never.

Gasping for breath he slumped against a locker. The laughter floated out of the kindergarten, filling the hallway.

"I'm done for," he moaned. "I can never show my face at this school again."

Suddenly he felt a slap on the shoulder. "Great!" said Henry. "Those kids loved your speech. And your pants trick was super. We'll do it again for the first graders."

"Are you kidding! I was never so embarrassed in my whole life. I'm never speaking again. To anyone." He tore off his blue star and handed it to Henry. "Here. I'm dropping out."

Henry's mouth flopped open. "But you can't quit. Do you want Zack to win? Do you want him to get rid of the Creepy Creatures?"

"Zack couldn't do that," said Melvin.

"Don't be so sure," said Henry. "Besides. You just need a few more speaking lessons. I'll teach you everything I know. Trust me."

"Trust you! I thought you said you and Mr. Libby were friends. I thought you were going to speak up for me."

"How did I know the kids would be such scaredy-cats?" said Henry. He tipped his hat back on his head. Then he shrugged his shoulders. "What could I do?"

Melvin shook his head. "I'm sorry. I can't give any more speeches. I'm terrible."

Henry pinned the blue star back on Melvin's shirt. "You're not terrible. You just don't believe in yourself. When you do that, you'll become a great speaker."

"Not unless I can wear the mask," Melvin said.

Henry cleared his throat and changed the subject. "Come to the clubhouse after school. We're going to work on your signs."

"My signs?" said Melvin.

"The signs we're going to put up at school," said Henry. "Your Purdy-for-president signs."

"Don't waste your time," said Melvin. "I'll never get through that speech on Friday."

Henry tapped Melvin on the nose. "Believe in yourself. Zack says you're a chicken. Prove him wrong."

"Zack doesn't say I'm a chicken. He says I'm a cluck-cluck."

Henry tapped Melvin's little nose. "But you're not. Are you?"

Melvin bit at his lip. He thought about how the kindergartners had laughed. What if something like that happened in front of the whole school?

"Well?" said Henry. "Speak up! What are you?"

Melvin looked as if he were going to cry. "Cluck-cluck," he whispered.

Chapter 4

◆

Strong Points

After school Melvin walked slowly to the Creepy Creatures Clubhouse. He was hoping no one would be there.

The clubhouse was in Rosa Dorado's garage. He knocked softly on the door.

"Who's there?" asked Rosa.

"Eyeballs and brains," said Melvin, giving the secret password.

"Come in," said Rosa, opening the door. "Make yourself uncomfortable."

Melvin stepped in and looked around. Even though he'd been there a thousand times, the place still gave him the shivers. Scary posters covered the walls. Three plastic skulls sat on a table in the back. Hanging from the ceiling, above a long green couch, a big hairy spider twisted slowly on a string.

"We've been waiting for you," said Henry. He was standing behind the couch, still wearing his top hat. Suddenly he pulled up a big white poster. It said, VOTE FOR PURDY! NO ONE IS BETTER THAN MELVIN AT

"Pretty neat, huh?" said Henry. "Well, what do you think?"

Melvin squinted. He read the poster for a second time. Then a third.

"I don't get it," he said. "No one is better than me at what?"

"That's what we're going to find out. Today," said Henry.

"I got this book at the library," said Rosa. She stepped forward. In her hand was a thick blue book. On the cover it said: *How to Win a School Election.*

"Does it say how to give a speech?" asked Melvin. "I hope so."

"I haven't gotten to that part yet," said Rosa. "The chapter I read was about making signs."

"It's really very simple," said Henry. "All we have to do is make a long list of your strong points."

"Everybody can make up to ten suggestions," said Rosa. "We'll pick out the best ones. Then put them on the sign."

"This will be a big help," said Henry.

"When you hear all your good points, you'll start believing in yourself."

Melvin smiled. "You really think so?"

"Trust me," said Henry.

"Okay," said Rosa, holding up a pencil. "Let's make a list of Melvin's strong points. And, please. Don't everyone shout at once."

Everyone looked around the room. But no one spoke. No one raised a hand. Rosa nervously chewed on the ends of her long black hair.

"Come on. Don't be shy," said Henry. "Tell us what makes Melvin so special."

Everyone stared at the floor. Melvin sat down on the couch. A little gray dog, Flip, was curled up in the corner. He was the club's mascot, and Melvin's best friend. Melvin began petting Flip, then he put him on his lap. Melvin didn't look up. He heard someone cough. But no one spoke. It was very embarrassing. For everyone.

"All right," said Henry, breaking the silence. "I'll start. Melvin's special point is that he is very . . . ummm, very . . . ummm, special!"

"Good point!" said Rosa. She wrote it down on a notepad.

"I know," said red-haired Ginger Stein. "Melvin is good with Flip. Does that count?"

Henry shook his head. "It would. But only if he was running for dog catcher."

After ten minutes no one else had thought up anything. Melvin felt like running away. He chewed nervously on his thumb and looked around the room, searching for an open door.

"I have it," said Henry at last. "We've been doing this wrong. Melvin is the one that should tell us his strong points. He's the Melvin Purdy expert here."

Everyone thought that was a good idea.

"Melvin, go ahead," said Henry. "Tell us your strong points."

Melvin took a deep breath. "Well, I always try to do my best."

"Excellent," said Henry. He took a pen and wrote on the poster, HE'S THE BEST.

"And I help my mom with the dishes," he said. "She says I'm really good." He giggled. "Once I carried all the dishes from the table to the sink in one trip. And I didn't even drop one!"

"Perfect," said Henry. He wrote on the poster: CHAMPION DISH JUGGLER.

"Anything else?" asked Rosa.

"I try to keep my word," he said. "If I say I'll do something, I'll do it."

"That will get you elected right there,"

said Henry. On the bottom of the poster he wrote: PURDY DELIVERS! IF HE SAYS IT, HE'LL DO IT!

Henry stood back and admired the sign.

"Pretty neat, huh?" he said.

Melvin winced. "You don't think it exaggerates too much, do you?"

"Are you kidding?" said Henry. He patted Melvin on the shoulder. "My boy, this poster is your ticket to success."

In fact, the poster was about to be a one-way ticket to disaster.

Chapter 5

◆

Promises, Promises

The next day Henry brought the poster to class.

"We'll put this up in the cafeteria," he told Melvin. "Everyone will see it at lunch."

"That's a very nice poster," said Ms. Hatfield. She had on her Wednesday tennis shoes. Low tops, covered with blue and yellow flowers. "Champion dish juggler. What's that?"

"Melvin carried all the dishes from the table to the sink in one trip," said Rosa. "It's one of his strong points."

"I guess a president needs to be good with dishes," said Ms. Hatfield. She scratched her chin. "But I'm not sure why."

"Me neither," said Melvin. "It was Henry's idea."

Henry took off his top hat and bowed.

"A brilliant idea, if I say so myself," he said. "Since Melvin doesn't like speaking, we're going to let the poster speak for him."

Ms. Hatfield pointed a finger at Melvin. "But Friday you'll have to talk at the assembly," she said. "Have you been working on your speech?"

Melvin rubbed his fist against his cheek. "I get the shivers just thinking about that speech."

"You'd better start practicing," said Ms. Hatfield. "Everyone who is running for president has to speak."

"I'm hoping I can wear my mask," said Melvin.

"I'm sure you'll need special permission," said Ms. Hatfield.

"Permission from you?" asked Melvin hopefully.

"No, from the principal, Mr. Gray," said Ms. Hatfield.

"The Monster of the Year is the only one who can give that speech," said Melvin. "He's much braver than me."

"The Monster of the Year is you," said Ms. Hatfield. "Don't be so afraid. We're all behind you. Remember. Believe in yourself. If you think you can do it, you can."

Melvin smiled and nodded. But inside he was thinking, "I can't do it."

For the rest of the morning Melvin chewed on his thumb and tried to think about his speech. He knew he would begin with a joke. Then he would tell everyone his strong points. Maybe he would end with a joke. Thinking about the speech made him nervous. He couldn't get his mind off of Friday. Finally, at eleven-thirty, a smell came drifting down the hall that made him forget his worries. It was the smell of chili. Lunch.

"Ummmm," he said, sitting back in his chair. "Chili dogs. My favorite."

When the bell rang, Melvin grabbed a bag holding the Monster of the Year mask. He felt nervous when he didn't have it with him. Then he hurried down the hall to the cafeteria.

He was first in line. Mrs. Ames, the cook, was wearing a black net over her hair. Melvin thought it looked like a spiderweb. Mrs. Ames smiled and give him two chili dogs.

"It's hard work running for president," she said. She read the message on Melvin's blue star, then said, "Enjoy lunch. It's a purdy good one today."

Melvin smiled. "It's my favorite," he said.

34

Melvin remembered how his Monday lunch had been ruined. He didn't want that to happen again. He found a table way in the corner. He put the bag with the mask down on the table. Then he sat down.

"Aha! There you are!" said Henry, suddenly appearing at his side. "We'll put the sign up next to the new president."

Before Melvin could say, "Leave me in peace," Henry had tacked up the poster. A second or two later Zack Morton showed up with his own poster.

He pinned it to the wall right next to Melvin's poster. Zack's poster said, VOTE FOR ME. OR ELSE. Under the words was a drawing of Zack holding up his fist.

"I thought I told you to drop out," said Zack, leaning in till he was nose to nose with Melvin. "Maybe you're not a cluck-cluck after all. Maybe you're just stupid."

"Make like the invisible man and disappear," said Henry. "Can't you see the next president is eating?"

Zack snorted and looked at Melvin's poster.

"What does this mean? The best champion dish juggler," he said.

Henry laughed. "Boy, you don't know anything, do you? Melvin is world famous. He's the greatest."

"The greatest cluck-cluck!" said Zack. He got nose to nose with Henry. For a second it looked as if there might be a fight. Everyone in the cafeteria stopped what they were doing. They all looked to see what was going to happen.

"All right," said Zack. He put his hands on his hips. "Let's see Melvin juggle some dishes."

Melvin shook his head. "Henry is exaggerating," he said. "I really don't . . ."

Zack tapped the poster. "It says here that Purdy delivers. When he says he'll do something, he does it."

"That's one of his strongest points," said Henry. He took off his hat and waved at the crowd in the lunchroom. "Purdy delivers!" he shouted. "That's why he'll make such a great president!"

"But, Henry," said Melvin.

"Melvin Purdy claims he can juggle," said Zack, shouting across the cafeteria. "He also says he does what he says." Zack folded his arms across his chest. "All right, big shot, grab some dishes. Do your stuff."

Melvin gulped. "But I can't really . . ."

"You see that?" said Zack. "He doesn't keep his promises."

All the students began talking. Zack was right. Melvin was about to break his word.

"You've got to juggle some dishes," whispered Henry. "Everyone is looking."

"He's a cluck-cluck. Isn't he?" said Zack.

Henry put his hands under Melvin's arms and stood him up. "Melvin Purdy delivers," said Henry. He gave Zack a dirty look. "He keeps his promises."

Melvin felt dizzy. The whole school was looking. Henry quickly grabbed four dirty plastic plates off the table. All the plates were loaded with gobs of chili.

"But, Henry," whined Melvin. He rubbed his fist against his cheek. "At home I just carried the dishes. Please. I'm not a juggler. I'm just Melvin Purdy."

Henry slapped a hand against his cheek. What Melvin had said gave him an idea. He grabbed the bag on the table. The monster-mask bag.

"Put on the mask," said Henry. "Maybe Melvin Purdy can't juggle. But the Monster of the Year can do anything."

Melvin grinned. Quickly he put on the mask. Zack gasped and stepped back.

"Out of my way!" said Melvin. With the mask on he was a changed person. "Stand back. Ladies and gentlemen. Presenting the world's greatest dish juggler. Me!"

Everyone was standing now. Mrs. Ames wondered what was going on. She stepped out from behind the counter. Just then Melvin threw up the first dish.

"Hey!" she shouted.

But before she could yell it again, three more plates shot into the air.

For a moment the plates hung above the ground like flying saucers. Melvin had never juggled plates before. Neither had the Monster of the Year.

"Catch them!" cried Henry.

Melvin scooted under one of the dishes.

Kerplop! A load of chili landed on his head.

Kerplop! Some more landed on the floor.

"Ha! Ha!" laughed Zack. "Some champion!"

Kerplop! Kerplop! the last two plates landed on Zack. A hunk of chili hit right on his head. Another hunk plowed into his neck.

"Oh, yuck!" said someone.

"What is going on!" demanded Mrs. Ames, charging across the room.

Melvin's mouth flopped open. A bit of chili slid through a hole in the mask and into his mouth. It was the only chili he was going to get for lunch.

A moment later he and Zack found themselves side by side, running out the door.

Just behind them came Mrs. Ames. She looked madder than anything.

Everyone in the cafeteria was laughing. Henry grinned and shouted out into the lunchroom, "Vote for Melvin on Friday. No matter if its promises or laughs, he always delivers!"

Suddenly the side door flew open. Melvin and Zack came running back into the cafeteria. They dashed between the tables, then out the other door. A moment later Mrs. Ames came barreling after them.

Everyone laughed some more.

Henry grinned. And tipped back his hat with his finger.

"Melvin sure made this lunchtime fun for everyone," he said. "I bet everyone votes for him now." He blew on his knuckles. Then he rubbed them on his chest. "Boy, I bet Melvin can't wait to thank me."

Suddenly a heavy hand clamped down on Henry's shoulder.

"Henry Potter. Come with me. You and Zack and Melvin are going to the principal." Henry looked up. It was Mrs. Ames. Under her other hand was Zack Morton. Melvin stood nearby, the mask half on, half off, his face. He glared at Henry and sneered. It wasn't the kind of look that said thank you.

40

Chapter 6

♦

House of Cards

Mrs. Ames marched the boys into the principal's office.

Mr. Gray, the principal, was busy. He was building a house of cards on his desk. He was almost finished with the fifth floor. When they walked in, he was carefully balancing one card on top of another.

"Mr. Gray," said Mrs. Ames, "I want to report a food fight."

Mr. Gray raised a hand. But he didn't look up. "Shhhh. Don't even breathe. I'm going for a record. I'm going to make a house of cards five stories tall."

"That's fine," said Mrs. Ames. "But these boys were throwing food. The cafeteria is a mess."

"It wasn't food fighting," said Henry. He

took off his hat and pressed it to his chest. "It was food juggling."

"Even worse," said Mrs. Ames. Her big bushy eyebrows were shaped like a sharp V. "So, what shall we do?"

"Well, we can't have food being thrown," said Mr. Gray.

"Certainly not!" said Mrs. Ames. And to help make her point she stomped her foot. Hard. The whole room shook. The house of cards teetered. But didn't fall.

Mr. Gray looked down at Mrs. Ames's foot. "Please, don't do that again," he begged, still not looking up.

Mrs. Ames sighed and tapped her foot loudly.

"Don't anybody move," said Mr. Gray. He bent over the house of cards. All you could see was the top of his bald head. "I'm going to be in the record books. Just this one last card. Then we'll call the TV stations and—"

"Mr. Gray," said Mrs. Ames, "I know your card house is important, but—"

"Shhhhh!" said Mr. Gray. "Nothing must disturb me."

Mrs. Ames put her hands on her hips. She glared at Mr. Gray. Then she looked at the three boys, one by one.

When she looked at Melvin, he pulled on the mask. He wasn't afraid of Mrs. Ames behind the mask. The Monster of the Year wasn't afraid of anything.

Mr. Gray balanced the card. It stayed. He grinned and rubbed his hands together.

"Aha! Five floors of cards! A record!" he said, admiring his work. "For three whole days I've been building this house. At last. I'm done. Call up the TV stations!"

Henry cleared his throat. He had suddenly remembered what Ms. Hatfield had said. How she said Mr. Gray would have to give Melvin permission to wear the mask at the assembly.

"Mr. Gray," he said, "could I bother you for a minute?"

Mr. Gray couldn't take his eyes off the house of cards. "What is it?"

"Melvin wants to wear a mask for his speech on Friday. Is that okay?" asked Henry.

"Mask?" said Mr. Gray. "What mask?"

"Why, the one he has on," said Henry. He jabbed Melvin in the ribs with his elbow. Then whispered to his friend, "This is perfect. Mr. Gray is in a great mood. He'll say okay for sure. Boy! Am I ever smart."

"Mask?" said Mr. Gray. He looked up

43

from his house. For a moment he seemed confused. He looked surprised to see so many people in his office. But he looked most surprised when he saw the Monster of the Year. His eyes opened wide. Then opened some more. For a second it looked as if they might pop.

"So! Can he wear it? Yes or no?" asked Henry.

For a moment Mr. Gray was frozen with fright. Then, as if he'd sat on a pin, he tried to leap up. "Eeeeee-yikes! Monster!" he screamed. Then a second later he yelled, "Ouch!" as his knee smashed into the desk. The house of cards shook. It looked as if it were being hit by an earthquake. A giant one.

"My house of cards!" screamed Mr. Gray.

Everyone gasped as the house came crashing down. Hearts and diamonds, clubs and spades, fluttered to the floor, like fall leaves.

"Oh, no ... Oh, no," cried Mr. Gray, grabbing for the cards as they floated by. "My house. My beautiful house."

"So!" said Henry. "Can he wear it?"

Mr. Gray's head came up from behind the desk. He glared at Henry. His eyes were on fire. His bald head glowed red. "Out!" he yelled, pointing to the door. "Go!"

44

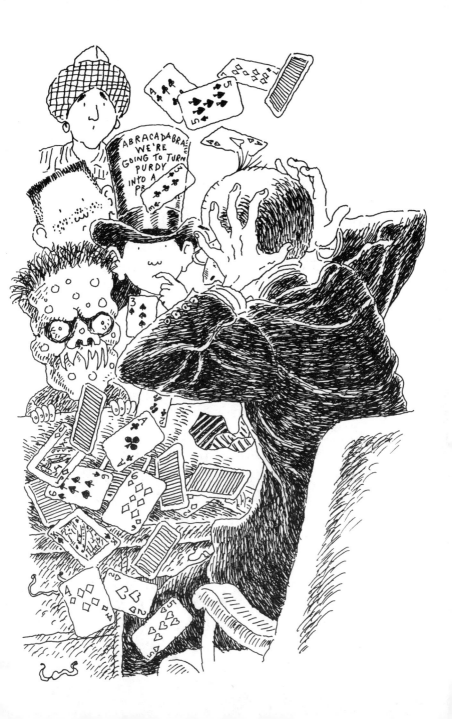

Henry winced. He pressed his hat onto his head and leaned forward. "Is that a yes or a no?"

"No! No! No!" he yelled. "Out!"

"I think Mr. Gray wants us to leave," said Melvin, pulling off the mask. "Let's scoot."

Mr. Gray looked like a volcano about to explode. Mrs. Ames and Zack hurried outside. Henry and Melvin followed.

"Don't ever bring that mask to school again!" Mr. Gray shouted after them. "Ever."

Melvin looked back just in time to see the door slam.

"Well," said Mrs. Ames, "it looks like your punishment will have to wait." Then, shaking her head, she marched off down the hall.

Henry blew on his knuckles. Then he rubbed them on his chest.

"You guys should thank me," he said. "I got us out of trouble."

"Thank you!" said Zack. "You got us into trouble in the first place."

"I'm not thanking you either," said Melvin. "Mr. Gray said I can't have the mask at school." He looked down at the mask in his hand. "Well, there goes my speech."

"Don't worry," said Henry. "I'll think of something."

"Forget it," said Melvin. "I can't stand up in front of the school on Friday. If I embarrass myself the way I did in the kindergarten, I'll have to drop out."

"Drop out of the race?" asked Henry.

"Nope," said Melvin. "Out of school."

Henry shot a look at Zack. The bully had a big grin on his face. "If Zack wins, he's going to make rules against the Creepy Creatures," said Henry. "You've got to speak. For the club."

"Sorry," said Melvin. He took off his paper star and handed it to Henry. "Here. I'm quitting."

Henry looked at the star and shook his head. "And I thought Purdy always delivered. That he always did what he said he was going to do."

"That was the Monster of the Year that did that," said Melvin. "You're looking at the Chicken of the Year."

"Melvin. Believe in yourself!" said Henry, grabbing his friend by the shoulders. "You're not a chicken."

"That's right," said Zack. "You're not a chicken. You're a scaredy-cat. That's even worse."

Melvin wanted to say something. But he couldn't. He knew that Zack was right.

Chapter 7

◆

Rosa's Hero

Melvin didn't bring his monster mask to school on Thursday. The Monster of the Year was not allowed on the school grounds. Mr. Gray had said so.

When class began, Melvin was in his seat, staring at his desk. And chewing on his thumb.

"Tomorrow is the big day," said Ms. Hatfield. She sat on the edge of her desk and clicked together her Thursday tennis shoes. Red ones. Low tops. "Aren't elections exciting! Why, I remember when I was a little girl, I ran for school treasurer. I had to give a speech and ..."

Ms. Hatfield's words drifted right over Melvin's head. Ms. Hatfield was always remembering things from when she was little. Boring things, mostly.

Anyway, Melvin didn't want to hear the word *election*. Or the word *speech*. It made him feel bad. He had dropped out. He had let down his friends in the Creepy Creature Club. He was a brave Monster of the Year. But he was a chicken Melvin Purdy.

"Melvin Purdy!"

Melvin shook his head and looked up.

"Melvin Purdy," said Ms. Hatfield, "haven't you been listening?"

"Ummmm." Everyone was staring. Melvin wished he had the mask. Wished he had something, anything, to hide behind.

Ms. Hatfield sighed. "I was just telling the class how proud I was of you."

Melvin tilted his head. His big ears got red. "You were? Why?"

"Because you're running for president," said Ms. Hatfield. "Because you're not afraid to stand up in front of the school and give a speech."

"Well," said Melvin, "actually, I . . ."

Ms. Hatfield shook a finger at Melvin. "Not many kids could do what you're doing."

"Zack Morton could," said Rosa. "He's running too. He said if he wins, he'll make rules against the Creepy Creatures. He won't let us have meetings at school."

"He won't let us wear our costumes to

49

school on special days either," said Ginger Stein. "He's mean. He better not win."

"I'm sure Melvin will give a great speech," said Ms. Hatfield. "He'll save the Creepy Creatures."

Melvin felt dizzy again. How could he tell Ms. Hatfield he had dropped out? He looked to Henry Potter for help. But Henry wasn't in a helping mood. He touched the brim of his hat and returned Melvin's look. Then folded his arms across his chest.

"Melvin will be our hero!" said Rosa, nearly jumping out of her seat. "He'll save us right at the last."

"No, I won't," mumbled Melvin.

"Huh?" said Ms. Hatfield.

"What?" said the class, leaning toward Melvin's desk. It was as if Melvin were a magnet. And everyone else were made of iron.

"I said I can't save the club," he said. "Yesterday I dropped out. Mr. Gray said I couldn't wear the mask. Only the Monster of the Year could give that speech. If I tried, I'd freeze up. Or worse."

"Worse?" said Ms. Hatfield.

"What if I peed in my pants?" said Melvin. The class giggled.

50

Ms. Hatfield got down from the desk. She walked over to Melvin and put her hand on his shoulder.

"Believe in yourself, Melvin Purdy. We all do," she said. "You're a good speaker. I want you to get up there tomorrow, and try."

Melvin shook his head and stared down at his desk.

"People always laugh at me," he said. "Even when I was little. Something always went wrong. Just like in the kindergarten class. Just like in the cafeteria."

"Tomorrow will be different," said Ms. Hatfield. "Tonight. Practice your speech. If you know it perfectly, the words will come out smoothly."

"You've got to do it for the club," said Rosa. The thought of Melvin dropping out had upset her so much, she began chewing on the ends of her hair.

Henry leaned across the aisle. He dropped the paper star onto Melvin's desk. "Put it on," he said. "We're all behind you."

Melvin looked down at the star. Then he looked around the room. Everyone was looking at him, and smiling. Maybe they did believe in him. Maybe they thought he really could do it!

"Okay," he said, pinning the star onto his shirt. "I'll try."

Everyone clapped.

"Come by the clubhouse after school," said Henry. "We'll help you practice your speech."

"Really?" said Melvin.

"We're all in this together," said Henry. "We're behind you one hundred percent."

Melvin nodded. He was glad everyone was behind him. But he wished someone was in front of him too. Someone like the big brave Monster of the Year.

Chapter 8

◆

Some Friends

After school Melvin walked to the Creepy Creature Clubhouse. All along the way he practiced his speech. He would start with the joke about the monster crossing the road. Then he would tell everyone his strong points. Finally, he would end with a joke.

"Maybe I can do it after all," he told himself. "With the Creepy Creatures behind me anything is possible."

When he got to the clubhouse, he saw that a lot of people were already there. Six bikes were outside. And he heard laughter coming from inside.

"Everyone is having a good time," he said. "I feel better already."

Melvin raised his hand to knock. But then, just before it came down, he heard someone say his name.

"Melvin Purdy can't do it!"

"Huh?" said Melvin, his hand still raised to knock.

"Can't do it. That says it all," came Rosa's voice.

"Why are they making fun?" said Melvin. He thought the Creepy Creatures were behind him one hundred percent. Not against him. He pressed one of his big ears to the door. And listened some more.

There were some more laughs. Then he heard Henry say, "He's nothing special. He's just . . ."

"Great. How true!" shouted Rosa, drowning out Henry's words.

"What a loser, huh?" came another voice.

"The worst," said someone else.

Melvin had heard enough. Now he knew the Creepy Creatures didn't believe in him. Didn't even like him!

He sighed, rubbed his fist against his cheek, and fought back the tears. Then, turning away from the door, he trudged off for home. After a while the shouts and laughter from the clubhouse faded away. But the terrible feeling that he was a loser wouldn't go away. He was certain, in fact, that it would never go away.

56

Chapter 9

◆

The Big Speech

All the way to school on Friday Melvin worked on his speech. Not the one he was going to give to the school. The one he was going to give to the Creepy Creatures.

"I quit!" he was going to say. "I heard you laughing behind my back. And I didn't like it. So I'm dropping out of the race. And out of the club too." Then, to make his point even stronger, he was going to add, "So there!"

He was still practicing the speech when he walked into the classroom. The first person he saw was Henry. He was looking into the mirror over the sink, adjusting his top hat.

"Melvin, my boy! Where were you yesterday?" said Henry, spotting Melvin in the mirror, then turning around. "We waited and waited at the club. But you never showed up."

"I'll tell you where I was," said Melvin. He tried to look angry. But he only looked scared. "Rats," he said to himself. "I wish I had the monster mask. The Monster of the Year would know how to yell at Henry."

"Well, never mind," said Henry. "We've got to get to the auditorium. The speeches start in ten minutes."

Melvin gulped. "Ten minutes . . . but—"

Ms. Hatfield was suddenly at Melvin's side, patting him on the shoulder. "I'm so very proud of you," she said. "I know you're going to give a wonderful speech."

"Speech?" said Melvin. But before he could say another word, Henry had him by the arm. And was moving him toward the door.

"Wish him luck, class!" shouted Ms. Hatfield.

"Good luck!" everyone cried. "You can do it!"

Melvin let himself be dragged away by Henry. "Good luck. Ha! They don't mean it. They think I'm a loser."

"I hope you've practiced," said Henry, leading Melvin down the hall. He glanced down at Melvin's pants. They were yellow

58

and green. Squares. He sighed. "I should have thought to bring you pants."

Melvin rolled his eyes. "You already did that once. Remember?"

There were lots of people backstage. Mr. Gray was there. Some students were fixing the lights. Other students were sitting on chairs. Suddenly Melvin felt a poke in the back.

"Hey, it's Mr. Cluck-Cluck!" said someone, laughing. Melvin turned around and saw Zack Morton. He had on his dirty leather jacket and a grin. Fluttering a hand in Melvin's face he asked, "Are you shaking?"

"Make like the breeze," said Henry. "Blow away."

Zack poked Henry in the chest. "You're looking at the next president, bigmouth. Better be nice. Or else."

Before Henry could reply, Zack gasped. Then ran off. Like a poked rabbit.

"What scared him?" wondered Henry.

Melvin pointed with his thumb. "That."

Henry looked up. He gasped too. Mr. Gray was pounding their way. And it was too late to run.

"Hello, Mr. Gray," said Henry, tipping his hat.

Melvin rubbed his fist against his cheek. "Sorry," he said.

"I want to see both of you in my office after lunch," said Mr. Gray. "Don't be late."

"Yes, sir," said Henry, saluting.

"Sorry again," said Melvin. Then, after Mr. Gray had left, he added, "We're really going to get it now."

"Don't worry about Mr. Gray. I can handle him," said Henry. "Worry about your talk."

"My talk!" said Melvin. For a moment he had forgotten all about his speech. And he had forgotten to tell Henry that he was dropping out. He looked around for the door. Mr. Gray was standing next to it. "Rats," he said. "I can't get away."

Fifteen minutes later the lights went down. And the curtain went up. All the teachers went, "Shhhhh!" And the program began.

Melvin leaned against the wall and stared at the floor.

"Practice hard," whispered Henry. "You go on soon. After Zack."

Melvin didn't reply. And he didn't practice his speech either. He was just thinking of one thing. How he was going to get off that stage. Out of the school. And back home.

One by one the students gave their speeches. Melvin chewed on his thumb and shuffled his feet on the floor. He hardly heard a word anyone said.

After about the fifth speech Henry whispered, "Are you ready?"

"Ready for what?" he said, looking up.

"To speak, of course."

"Speak! No way! Not after what happened yesterday," said Melvin.

"Yesterday?" said Henry. He wrinkled his lip. "What are you talking about?"

Melvin sighed. "I heard the Creepy Creatures talking at the club yesterday. I heard the mean things they said."

"Nobody said anything mean about you," said Henry. "Just the opposite."

"Don't lie," said Melvin. "I heard Rosa say I couldn't do it. And I heard you say that I was nothing special."

Henry laughed.

Melvin rubbed his fist against his cheek. "It's not funny."

Henry put a hand on Melvin's shoulder. "Rosa said that what you couldn't do was drop out. She said that the club was so important to you that you couldn't quit. She was proud of you."

"She was?" said Melvin.

"And you're right. I did say you weren't anything special. I said you were super special. But you must not have heard the end of the sentence."

"Someone else said I was a loser, and the worst," said Melvin.

"We were talking about Zack," said Henry. "Not about you. We were making signs."

"Signs?" said Melvin.

Onstage Zack had just started his speech. He was shaking his fist at the crowd. And yelling at them to vote for him.

Quietly, Henry led Melvin to the edge of the stage. Then they both peeked out from behind the curtain and looked at the crowd.

"There," said Henry, pointing to the back. "See the signs?"

Melvin squinted into the gloom. All along the back the Creepy Creatures had hung signs. One of them said, PURDY ISN'T ANYTHING SPECIAL.... HE'S SUPER SPECIAL. Another said, IF MELVIN CAN'T DO IT, NO ONE CAN. And the biggest one of all read, MELVIN PURDY, WE BELIEVE IN YOU.

Melvin's mouth dropped open. The Creepy Creatures really did like him!

"And another thing," said Zack. "Elect me president and you won't see any dumb monster costumes at this school. Vote me

in. And you'll vote the Creepy Creatures out. Let's give those cluck-clucks the big heave-ho!"

When Melvin heard the words *Creepy Creatures,* he turned his attention to Zack. He didn't like the way he was talking about his friends. His friends who believed in him.

"So," said Henry, "are you still afraid to speak? Afraid to talk without the mask?"

Melvin didn't reply. He was mad. Mad at Zack.

"Vote for me," said Zack, ending his speech. He waved to the crowd. "Let's say good-bye to the Creepy Creatures!"

Before Zack was off the stage, Melvin was on it.

When the Creepy Creatures saw Melvin, they cheered. But Melvin didn't seem to hear. He was madder than anything.

"That Zack," he said. "He's like a vampire. A pain in the neck!" Everyone laughed at Melvin's joke.

The laughter caught Melvin by surprise. He squinted and looked out into the crowded auditorium. Then gulped. Without thinking, he'd come onstage. Then started his speech.

For a moment he froze. But then he remembered that everyone had laughed at his joke. And he saw the sign in the back too. The one that said the Creepy Creatures believed in him. He drew in a deep breath. Then plunged ahead.

"Vote for me. I'll keep the laughs coming," he said. "I want school to be fun."

Everyone clapped.

He listened to the cheers and smiled. By golly, he did believe in himself! He had run out onstage because he was mad at Zack. But now he was glad to be speaking. It was even fun.

"I'll keep all my promises," he said. "You can depend on Purdy." Then he waved to the students. "If you want a good president, vote for me! Purdy, purdy please!"

Everybody laughed and clapped. Melvin waved and blew everyone kisses. Then he walked off the stage. And into Henry's arms.

"Melvin! You were great."

"It was nothing," said Melvin. He blew on his knuckles. Then rubbed them on his chest. "Speaking is easy. All you have to do is believe in yourself."

Chapter 10

♦

Extra Help

Later that morning the students voted.

"Attention!" said Mr. Gray over the loud-speaker. "Time to announce the new school president."

Ms. Hatfield's room got super quiet. Rosa chewed on the ends of her hair. Ms. Hatfield crossed her fingers. And Melvin shut his eyes.

"We had a very close race between Zack Morton and Melvin Purdy," said Mr. Gray. "Zack Morton had ninety-eight votes. And Melvin Purdy had ... Whoa ... Oh, whoops!" There was a long pause. You could hear something crash. Then Mr. Gray came back on and said, "Sorry. My chair just tipped over."

"Go on!" said Henry. "Tell us."

And he did.

"Melvin Purdy had one hundred and six. Melvin is our new president."

Ms. Hatfield's room exploded. Everyone jumped up and ran over to Melvin's desk.

"You did it!" said Ms. Hatfield. "I'm so proud."

"I didn't do it," said Melvin. He couldn't stop grinning. "The Creepy Creatures did it. They made me believe in me."

Henry made a fist and hit Melvin on the shoulder. "What a team. Stick with me. We're going places. All the way to the White House."

Before Melvin could answer, the loud-speaker came on again.

"Melvin Purdy, report to the principal's office, at once. You, too, Henry Potter."

Melvin sighed. "We're going places, all right. Thanks to you."

Henry smiled. Then he made a face. "Sorry," he said.

Henry and Melvin took their time getting to Mr. Gray's office.

"He's waiting," said the secretary, Mrs. Post. "Go inside."

Henry and Melvin stepped into Mr. Gray's office. To their surprise they saw another house of cards sitting on his desk. It was just like the other one, five stories tall.

"Wow!" said Melvin.

"Just look at that," said Henry. He walked

over to the house of cards. Then said, "I couldn't have done a better job myself."

"I didn't give up," said Mr. Gray. "And neither did you, Melvin. You see, that's all it takes to succeed."

"Great advice. Let me take my hat off to you," said Henry. And he reached up and swept the top hat off his head.

"Henry! Look out!" cried Melvin.

But Melvin's words came too late. Henry's hat was already smashing into Mr. Gray's house of cards.

"Eeeee-yikes!" yelled Melvin. He put his hands to his head as he watched the house start to tip.

"Whooops!" yelled Henry. "Oh, no!"

The house went over on its side. But it didn't fall apart! Not a card fluttered off. Mr. Gray smiled. He picked up the house with one hand and set it back up straight.

Melvin and Henry stood frozen like statues, their mouths open.

"It pays to never give up," said Mr. Gray. "But it also pays to have some help. Melvin, you won because the Creepy Creatures stuck together. And my house didn't fall down because it was stuck together too." He grinned. "With glue."

Melvin gasped. "So that's how you did it!"

"Wow. You were sure lucky," said Henry.

"You mean you were sure lucky," said Mr. Gray.

Henry looked at the house and gulped. Mr. Gray couldn't have been more right.

Monster Jokes

Hi! It's Melvin Purdy again. If you want to give a good speech, start things off with a joke. Perhaps you might want to try one of these. They're guaranteed to get you a standing ovation every time.

What is the best way to talk to a monster?
Long distance

Dracula: Is the Invisible Woman cute?
Frankenstein: Yep. She's like nothing you've seen before.

What kind of shots do ghosts like best?
Boo-ster shots

Movie Director: How would you like to play King Kong in my next movie?
Actor: No way! What do you want to do? Make a monkey out of me?

What do dragons have that no one else has?
Baby dragons

71

Please, Nurse, I've got to see a doctor. I keep thinking I'm the Invisible Man.
Hey! Who said that?

What do you say to a giant ape that wins the lottery?
Kong-gratulations!

Little Frankenstein: Daddy, can I have some money? I want to buy a pound of birdseed.
Frankenstein: But, son, you don't own a bird.
Little Frankenstein: I know. That's why I want the birdseed. So I can grow one!

What kind of baseball games do monsters like best?
Doubleheaders

Troll #1: Where are you living these days?
Troll #2: At the bottom of a well. Drop in sometime.